Armful of Memories

Peter Jan Honigsberg

illustrated by
Tony Morse

RDR Books
Oakland, California

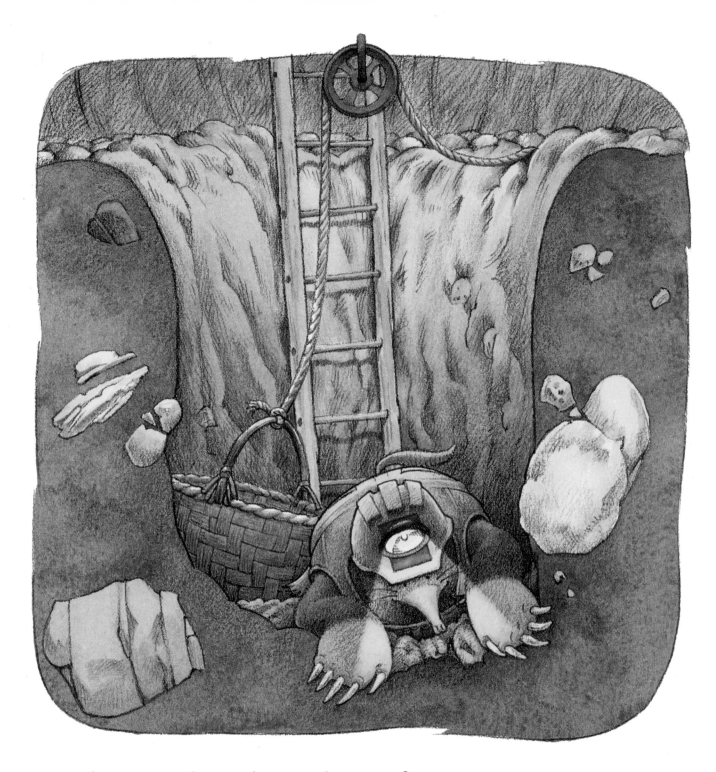

Newberry Mole is always digging for treasure. He wants to get rich quick.

"Today, I'll tunnel right below my home," he decides. "Maybe, I'll find treasure there."

He shovels and shovels. Suddenly, he tumbles into a hole.
Plop! He brushes himself off and looks around. He's in a
room with a chair, table, and bed. There are photographs on
the walls. "Hmm," he thinks. "Those pictures seem familiar."
He crawls up closer. "Wow! They're pictures of my family.

Look, there's my grandma and grandpa holding me when I was a baby. And there is me with my grandma and grandpa and my parents on a trip to the Grand Tunnel." Then he remembers, "This is where my grandmother and grandfather used to live."

Newberry searches the other rooms, hoping to discover more memories of his grandparents and the rest of his family. He opens a kitchen cabinet and finds salad plates, soup bowls,

and jars. On the stove he sees his grandma's old cooking pot. "That's the pot Grandma always used to make yummy potato bug stew for us on cold winter nights," he remembers.

He wanders out to the toolshed and spots his grandpa's tools and toolbox. There's also a picture of Newberry's grandparents taking him on the Daredevil Mud Slide at the amusement park.

"It's my lucky day to have fallen into my grandparents' old home," cheers Newberry. "I'm finding so many special photographs and other old things. I bet other animals would like this neat old stuff too. I'm sure I could sell all these treasures and get lots of money."

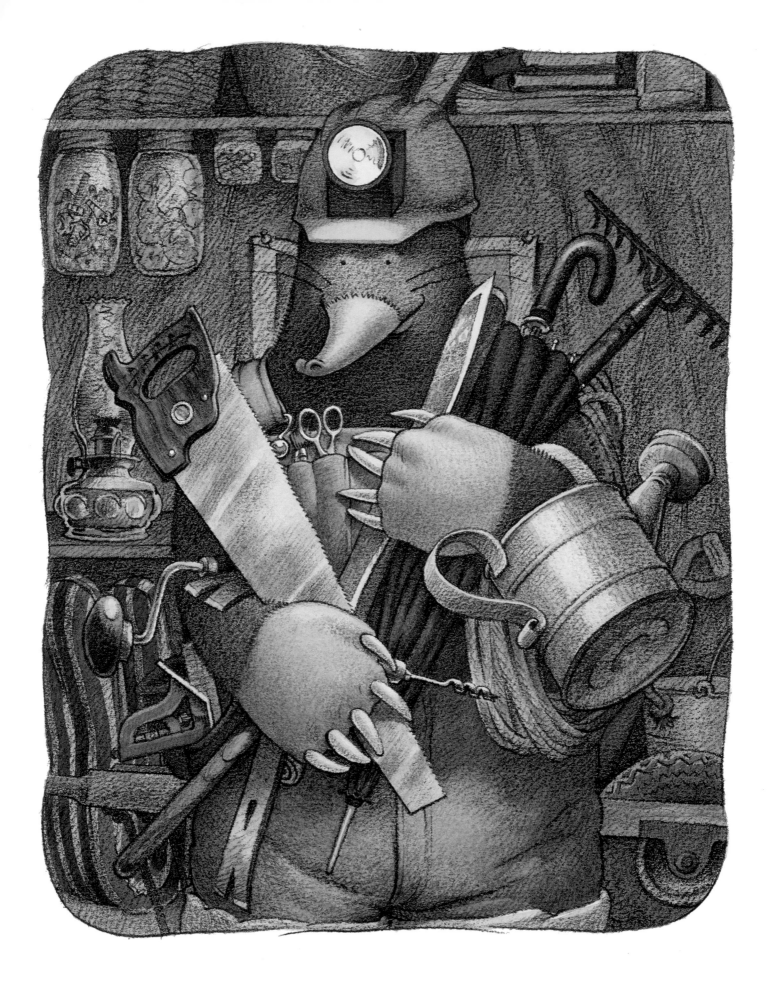

Newberry Mole carries his newly found riches up to his house.
The next day, he puts up signs announcing a yard sale.

From a branch, Squirrel spots the signs and dashes down
to see what Newberry is selling. "I could use those jars to

store my nuts," Squirrel thinks. So he buys them. Margaret
Bunny, who is out strolling, passes by Newberry's yard.
"These are pretty salad plates," she says. "My mother could
use them for our lettuce and carrots. I'll buy them for her."

Beaver purchases Newberry's father's tools. "These will help me build another home," Beaver declares.

As the Raccoon family proudly parades by, the children call, "Mom, Dad, can we have new finger bowls to wash our

hands in before we eat?"

"Sure," says Mama Raccoon.

Newberry can't believe it. "I've made so much money," he exclaims. "And I still have these photographs to sell too."

Later in the day, Fox comes along. "What are you selling today?" he asks.

"Well, not much is left," Newberry replies. "But I do have these photographs."

Fox thinks, "The photos of the Mole family don't mean much to me, but the picture frames are very pretty. I could sell the frames in my store. And maybe someone will want the photos too."

So Fox buys all the Mole family photographs and their frames.

"I sold everything," Newberry shouts. "I'm rich, I'm rich."

That night, Newberry Mole has a dream. He dreams that he is on a picnic with his parents and grandparents. After they finish eating their strawberries, caterpillars, and wiggle-worm sandwiches, they decide to go for a boat ride on the lake.

"It's so nice to have a day off," Newberry thinks, "and not have to dig a tunnel in the murky-dark ground. How perfect."

But in his dream, Newberry suddenly realizes that he cannot see the faces of his grandmother and grandfather. Their faces are a blur.

Newberry wakes up with a start. "Oh no, I sold all my photographs to Fox. Without the pictures, how will I remember how Grandma and Grandpa looked? What will I do?"

In the morning, Newberry quickly gets dressed, and races over to Fox's shop.

"Oh, Mr. Fox," Newberry worries, "I made a terrible mistake. I sold you all my photographs and now I have no memories of how my grandparents looked. Can I please have the pictures back? You can keep the frames."

"I'm sorry, but you're too late," Fox chuckles. "I sold all of them, and made lots of money too."

"But how could you?" shrieks Newberry. "Who would want photos of my family?"

"Someone came in only a while ago and bought them all," Fox replies. "She really wanted them."

"Oh no," Newberry groans. "Now, I'll never be able to remember how my grandparents and family looked." He slinks out of Fox's store. That night, he cries himself to sleep.

A week later, he gets a letter.

Dear Newberry,

I was at Fox's store last week and saw all of the Mole family photographs for sale. I bought them all, but he charged me a lot of money.

Do you have any idea who sold him the pictures? He wouldn't tell me. I can't imagine why someone would sell all of our family photographs and memories!

Love,
Aunt Clara Mole

The letter cheers him up. Maybe he can get the photographs back! He dashes to Aunt Clara's home.

"I sold the photographs, Aunt Clara. I wanted money," he sighs. "But now since you have them, can I have them back? I didn't know I was selling all my memories."

"Slow down, Newberry," advises Aunt Clara. "I paid a lot of money to Fox for those pictures. I couldn't afford them, but I didn't want someone else to have the Mole family photos. You will have to help me pay for them."

"How much, Aunt Clara?" asks Newberry, as he counts out his money. "This is all I have," showing her all the money from his yard sale.

"Well, that only covers one-half of what I paid Fox," Aunt Clara replies. "But since I would like some of the photographs myself, I'll keep half, and you can have the rest."

Feeling happy and sad at the same time, Newberry hands over every penny he has. Then, Aunt Clara invites Newberry for beetle crackers and milk, and he tells her about his adventures finding the Mole family treasures.

That night at home, Newberry admires the photographs. He is no longer rich, but he has his pictures of his family. At bedtime, he tucks pictures of his grandparents under his pillow. Then he goes to sleep.

"If I dream of Grandma and Grandpa tonight," Newberry thinks to himself, "at least I know that when I wake up, I will be able to remember their faces clearly. I may have no money, but now I will always have my memories of my family with me. My memories are my real treasures."